DR. S. K. BURKMAN

Squeaky Hatchling

The Dragon Doc Tales: A Novelette

The Dragon Doc Tales series is dedicated to veterinarians the world over. To my colleagues who struggle to persevere in a profession that is often as overwhelming and heartbreaking as it is uplifting and gratifying, I see you. Your patients are grateful to you, and so am I.

Contents

1

A Rough Landing

Dragons usually snorted and snuffled around me, but I knew they could roar. While I was on backpacking trips deep in the mountains, I'd heard them do it: thunderous, menacing bellows that made the hair rise up on the back of my neck. I didn't know that these formidable creatures could also squeak. But then, if I told you everything I knew about dragons, I'd have told you that time and experience have constantly changed my understanding of them. Just when I thought I'd seen it all, something new and strange would come along, some unexpected challenge to conquer. That's exactly what happened on one memorable Saturday evening.

My daughter, Ember, and I were the only ones home for the weekend. My husband was traveling on business and wouldn't be home until Monday. In hindsight, it was the perfect setup for a mother-daughter adventure.

I'd made cookies for the veterinary clinic staff on Friday and promised Ember I would bring home the leftovers. Honestly, I was surprised that there *were* any leftovers, although I'd made over two dozen. Veterinarians and staff churned through frightening amounts of sugar and caffeine on busy days; an unhealthy routine, but it kept us going.

But in my hurry to leave and pick up Ember from school, I'd made an unforgivable mistake, at least to a third grader: I'd forgotten the cookies. And, as physically and mentally exhausting as the week had been, setting foot in the clinic before my next workday was the last thing I wanted to do. I'd tried to distract her with a fast food dinner and ice cream, but the diversion only worked for one night. By Saturday, she had caught on.

"Mom, you promised!" Ember whined, glaring at me reproachfully from her seat at the dinner table.

"Yes, I did, and I'm sorry I forgot, but it's getting late tonight. How about we pick them up tomorrow?"

"You promised to bring them home last night. Tonight is closer to last night than tomorrow is."

Laughing, I had to acknowledge she had a point. So, despite my reluctance, we drove to the clinic after dinner to pick up the dregs of Friday's sugar high for dessert.

It was a blustery, chilly November evening, soon enough after the time change that darkness pounced late in the afternoon, and all my staff complained about it, as if it didn't happen every year. Ember and I shivered as we walked the short distance between the car and the back door, illuminated harshly beneath the security lamp that mercilessly highlighted every scrape, scratch, and crack on the back of the old building.

Nestled at the edge of a residential neighborhood, the clinic was an imposing cube of cinder blocks with a hopeful, modern stucco facade framed by large, stately trees. Behind it lay the clinic parking lot, just off the neighboring alley and surrounded by houses with their blinds and curtains drawn tight. This was where I typically encountered our more unconventional patients. Ostensibly, we only treated small animals; we routinely saw dogs and cats and the occasional ferret, rabbit, or rodent. What few people knew was that we also saw rather unusual patients on the side: dragons.

Years before, I'd inadvertently been introduced to a wounded dragon and had helped her as best I could. I'd thought the whole experience was a product of my imagination — until real, live dragons had started seeking me out for veterinary care. When the first few dragons accosted me at my clinic, I'd been terrified, and had started questioning everything I thought I'd known was real. With time, however, I'd become more comfortable around the dragons. Patient by patient, I'd treated them in secret, learned dragon anatomy and physiology, made many mistakes, and endured quite a few calamities. I'd been bruised, burned, blasted with horrid-smelling breath weapons, and frightened out of my wits countless times, but I'd helped many dragons along the way. Nearly two decades later, even though dragons appearing at my clinic was old news, they remained daunting patients, and I respected the dangers involved in treating them.

Ember and I retrieved the cookies from the break room, slipping the container into a plastic grocery bag to carry. Mission accomplished, we left the clinic — and our evening abruptly became much more interesting.

Typically, I didn't hear dragons when they arrived. Instead, I'd glimpse them lurking in the shadows between the trees, or spy a fleeting movement at the edge of the building — some hint that one had arrived in need of help. They landed so quietly it was uncanny. Usually, that is.

This one landed with an uncoordinated crash on the lawn next to the parking lot, nearly skidding into the trunk of a large elm tree. A lower branch broke with a sharp *snap* and ricocheted off the dragon's spikes as it tumbled to the ground. The creature slid to a stop merely fifty feet from where Ember and I were exiting, cookies in hand — oddly enough, not the strangest way I've encountered a dragon before. After almost twenty years of working with dragons, I barely flinched at the surprise appearance.

Ember, however, jumped and grabbed my arm. "Mom, what is that?"

Quickly surveying the neighboring houses, I was relieved that all the curtains remained closed despite the crash. The train yard several blocks away generated all manner of crashes and booms, and the locals seemed resigned to loud noises.

"Uh oh, kiddo, I think we've got a sick dragon to contend with."

My daughter's shock quickly turned to excitement. "Cool! Can I help?"

"I'd rather you stayed at a safe distance."

"Awww, but Mom—"

Suddenly, a strange, high-pitched sound interrupted Ember's protests. A snort, then an odd squeal emanated from the direction of the dragon. The sound was low in volume, but annoyingly shrill. *What on earth is that?*

"Stay here, okay? You can be my lookout. And keep the cookies safe." People occasionally walked through the alley, and though thankfully fencing and bushes shielded the lawn, they didn't completely obscure it. My partner and staff knew about the dragons, but the general public did not, and I wanted to keep it that way.

A high-powered shop light hung just inside the back door for exactly these kinds of situations. I grabbed it and cautiously approached the dragon, which hadn't moved after landing, nearly invisible in the shadows beneath the trees. A strange, muffled whistle sounded as I approached, followed by another snort. Scanning from side-to-side, I verified there were no humans nearby other than my small cookie-loving sentry. Then, I shone the light over the dragon.

No, not just one dragon. Dragons, two of them: a mother and hatchling.

I cringed. The mother dragons had developed an irritating habit years before: no matter how much I protested, they'd dump their sick or injured babies on me and fly off the moment their hatchlings were in my hands. Then, the babies would be mine for days, often considerably longer than they needed to be hospitalized. The dragon mothers seemed to inherently trust me to care for their babies, which I found both touching and maddening, not to mention expensive; once they were feeling better, the hatchlings churned through food. Long ago, I'd sunk an inheritance into a trust fund to defray the costs of dragon medicine, and having to leverage the fund to feed perfectly healthy hatchlings was infuriating.

Both mother and baby were a stunning shade of crimson red, so vivid that they would have attracted far too much attention if it weren't for their highly evolved camouflage mechanisms. The mother weighed at least seven thousand pounds, larger than my Volkswagen car, with an impressive array of horns and spikes from her face to the tip of her tail. Three sets of ivory-colored horns curled gracefully away from the back of her head, the primary pair longer than my arms, the next pair a bit shorter, and a third set just beginning to emerge. Based on the number and size of horns, I concluded that she was considerably more mature than most of the mother dragons I'd encountered. I wondered whether she had hatched and raised other baby dragons.

Rows of dark magenta spikes coursed from a small cluster at the tip of the mother dragon's muzzle, over her face and jaws, and neatly between her horns, growing larger and more intimidating as they snaked down her spine and tail, culminating in a dense array of sharp spicules over her spade-shaped tail tip. Her scales were shaped like blunt diamonds, with an iridescence that sparkled and shimmered under the harsh glare of my shop light. The crimson hue over her dorsum, wings, and limbs faded to opalescent ivory plates that protected her chest and abdomen. Both wings sported some nicks and small tears in the leathery, blood-red hide. This, combined with the missing talon on one rear foot, and the handful of fractured spikes along her spine and tail, also suggested the dragon's advanced age.

The mother turned to acknowledge me, peering with eerie, fiery eyes that complemented her hide and scales. The vermilion irises blazed like twin Eyes of Sauron around dark scalloped pupils.

Left breathless by the dragon's formidable size and beauty, I watched as she turned back to her hatchling.

"Ember," I called over my shoulder. "Are you doing okay?"

"Yes, Mom. That's a really big dragon."

Baby dragons often varied from the colors and patterns of their parents, but this one appeared quite similar to his mom. Bright ruby scales adorned the hatchling's entire body, with stubby new spikes emerging over his face, spine, and tail. The back of his head sported tiny cherry-red horn buds; I suspected these might turn cream-colored as the dragon matured. His nose was blunted and his forehead broad, and he blinked with wide flame-hued eyes that looked like the cartoon versions of

Tolkien's villain.

During the fall, I sometimes glimpsed red dragons in the wild, along with orange and yellow ones. They let their defenses down just a bit when they could so easily blend in with the autumn leaves. However, no colorful foliage remained this late in the season to hide this pair. Even after all my years of treating dragons, I was amazed how well they were able to disguise themselves, particularly with coloration as vivid as this pair. How they managed it, I had mainly theories. Similar to chameleons, dragons possessed chromatophores, but the physiology of their disguises went beyond that. They were so talented at concealment, I could have dismissed their abilities as magic, but I knew there had to be scientifically sound explanations. I just hadn't figured them all out — yet.

When dragons wished to hide, they remained motionless, fading into their surroundings to near invisibility. Rapid and thorough color change was part of the process, but they also appeared less substantial, as if half their cells became transparent. If hidden dragons needed to move, the margins of their disguises rippled, but the vague distortion was difficult to recognize as anything resembling a dragon. If anything, an observer might rub her eyes, squint, and wonder whether she should have her vision checked. However, the dragons' disguises weren't foolproof. I'd gathered that camouflaging themselves required focus and effort, and sometimes the dragons lacked both. Mythology depicted dragons as nearly infallible and indestructible, but in reality, they were sometimes distracted and clumsy.

My nose twitched at the dragons' acrid scent. Invisible or not, there was no hiding the smoky, bitter, foul odor of dragons. It smelled like I'd stumbled upon a family of skunks holding a backyard barbecue.

The hatchling was about the size of a Labrador retriever, just small enough that his mother had to carry him; he hadn't flown on his own. But he was big enough to resist her grip. Apparently the mother hadn't yet moved toward the clinic because she was busy wrestling her recalcitrant son, who writhed, thrashing his head and tail and clawing at her toes as she grasped him in her front claws. His little wings flapped in fury, slapping his mother's face. She grimaced in irritation and let go of his hind limbs to grab his wings, only for him to resort to kicking her.

The odd whistling noise sounded again, three times in succession, accompanied by a furious fit of squirming from the baby and a snort from the mother. The noise must have been coming from the hatchling, but I'd never heard such a sound from a dragon.

"What's going on with you, little one? Mama dragon, can you show me?"

The big red dragon paused her wrestling match with the wiggly hatchling long enough to turn my direction. Then, she plopped the ruby toddler on the grass in front of me. As he hit the ground, there was a muffled squawk, then what looked like a hard swallow. He swallowed again, and the squawk repeated, louder this time. The mother snorted at her baby and then looked at me.

"What the hell?"

Kneeling, I shone the light closer over the red hatchling, looking over his head and face, eyes, nostrils, and ear slits. He faced my direction, looking curiously at the light. I wasn't fond of being within the "strike zone" for fire. Babies started breathing fire within hours of birth, and they had less control over their flame emissions than adults. So, I shuffled farther to his side and away from his face. He started to turn as well, trying to follow the light.

"Nope, stay there so I can examine you—"

To my surprise, the mother dragon grasped her son with her great claw to keep him in place. She had stayed rather than immediately flying off, a refreshing change. I was grateful for her help, though I doubted she would stick around for long.

With the big dragon's claw holding the hatchling in place, I continued my exam. My stethoscope was in the clinic, so listening to his heart and lungs would have to wait. But he appeared to be a good weight, well-muscled, with wings and toes intact, shiny, healthy scales, and no broken spikes. Whatever was going on, it was an acute problem.

The hatchling extended his head and neck, swallowed, and squealed noisily. The sound was definitely coming from his mouth or throat. *Great.* I didn't love working closely with the fiery parts of a dragon, but for this, I would have to.

Sitting back on my heels, I considered how best to proceed. To get a good look in the hatchling's mouth, I'd have to use sedation; I could have coaxed an older dragon into opening its mouth wide, but not one this young. Ember's insistence on collecting the cookies was about to earn her an eventful evening.

"Well, little guy, looks like I need to sedate you so I can figure out where these strange noises are coming from. Are you going to stick around, Mama?" I looked pointedly at the mother dragon.

She regarded me for a few moments. "Stay," she said in a guttural, strained voice.

My eyebrows rose. I could never predict which dragons might talk to me. Speaking required effort, and I suspected that many dragons probably had the ability to speak — after all, they understood what I said to them — but chose not to.

"All right. I'm going to give your hatchling an injection to sedate him. Then I'll take him inside the clinic. I'm afraid you won't fit in the building."

She snorted in reply.

As I walked back toward the clinic and Ember, still stationed watchfully next to the back door, I considered which of my staff to call for help. Ideally, with a sedated patient, I needed another skilled set of hands.

"It's a baby dragon, right, Mom? She's so cute!"

"*He*, actually, and yes he is cute. But he has something wrong with him, and I need to call someone to help me with sedation."

"Please, Mom, I want to help."

I paused at the back door and turned back toward the dragons. They were once again shrouded in shadows beneath the trees, but not camouflaged. I could envision the hatchling, crouched on the grass in his mother's firm grip. He probably weighed about seventy pounds. I rarely had the luxury of weighing a dragon before I calculated drug dosages, but I had developed decent skills at estimating their body weight.

"Okay, kiddo, let's go inside, and you can help me set up while I call a technician to help."

Ember's eyes lit up at the prospect of helping me. "What about the dragons, though? Will they just… stay there?"

"Probably. I mean, I'm pretty sure they'll still be here somewhere. Just exactly where, I never know." After all these years of dealing with dragons, I still found them difficult to predict.

Finding a veterinary technician to assist turned out to be a fruitless endeavor that evening. "Jess? I'm sorry to bother you.

Is this the weekend you're in Boise?"

"Yeah, I'm driving back tomorrow. Why, what's up?"

I explained my dragon predicament. "What about Katie, do you know if she might be around this weekend?"

"Mommmm," Ember interjected in a stage whisper. *"I want to help!"*

"No, Katie, Becky, and Amara all went to the hot springs today. Pretty sure they're still there. Maybe call Dr. Beth?"

"Ah, that's right, I'd forgotten they were planning a hot springs trip. As cold as it is, I'm a little jealous… No, I really don't want to call Beth. She covered for me yesterday afternoon, and she worked this morning too. I'm not going to ask her down tonight, although I know she'd say yes."

"Mommmmmmm! I can HELP!" The stage whisper was growing in volume and insistence.

"So what are you going to do?"

"Ehh, I'll wing it. No pun intended. I'm sure I can manage. Plus I have an eight year-old aspiring assistant who's dying to help out."

The aspiring assistant hopped up and down with glee.

In truth, I had managed to do a lot of dragon medicine for years without any assistance, but that was before I started seeing so many hatchlings, and therefore before needing sedation so frequently to accomplish treatment. Adult dragons were typically cooperative — well, "cooperative" perhaps wasn't the right word, but they were usually amenable enough to my requests that I was able to get them diagnosed and treated. With some calamities along the way, true, but I'd survived and learned how to work around their challenges.

"Well, good luck. I wish I could be there to help."

"No, Jess, it's fine. I'm sorry to bug you on your day off." We said our goodbyes, and I ended the call.

My assistant was still bouncing up and down, pumping her fists with excitement. "I get to help! I get to help! I get to—"

"Hey, please calm down. First, don't interrupt me while I'm on the phone. Second, remember that dragons are wild animals. They are dangerous. Even the babies, even in a controlled situation, can hurt you. So you need to do *exactly* what I tell you to do, okay? And be extremely careful."

The bouncing ceased, and she adopted a serious expression, but her delight shone through. "Okay Mom. I promise I'll follow directions."

Ember had been around dragons her entire life, but she had never experienced them up close in a clinical situation. She loved them, and while I was confident in her ability to assist me to some extent, I knew she wasn't old enough to have quite enough respect or appreciation for the dragons' capacity to inflict harm to humans, not to mention the building and equipment. I would have to supervise her closely.

I recalled a conversation we'd had just the day before, when I'd asked her whether she ever talked about dragons at school.

"Yeah, sometimes," she'd said. "I don't really talk about your work, but I remember seeing a baby dragon in our back yard when I was little. He kept popping his head in and out of the bushes, like he was playing peek-a-boo. I think that's one of the earliest things I can remember."

Smiling and shaking my head, I recalled the same hatchling, his nose thick with snot from a respiratory infection. We'd called him Peek-A-Boo thanks to his game with Ember. His mother had the audacity to leave him at my house, then finally turned up at the clinic days later to take her baby home. By then, after several days of antibiotics, he was considerably less snotty, and quickly burning through my grocery budget. He consumed at least fifty dollars' worth of chicken thighs alone.

"So, what does your teacher say about the dragons?"

"She says I have a good imagination. She says the same thing to Keith. He says he has a pet elephant at home."

I laughed. "Really? Do you ever try to convince her that the dragons are real? And wait, does Keith really have an elephant?" A younger version of me would have assumed 'no,' but then, the same version wouldn't have believed that dragons existed.

"No. Mom, I know that most people don't get to see them. It's okay. And, no, I don't think Keith has an elephant."

"What do you think would happen if people knew that the dragons were real?" I had many thoughts on this subject, but I was curious to hear the perspective of my daughter, who hadn't yet lived long enough to adopt my cynicism.

She frowned in contemplation for a few moments. "I think that… people would just ruin it. And ruin them."

"Ruin? What do you mean by that?" Maybe my cynicism had rubbed off after all. I was taken aback and saddened by the realization, and yet proud of her perception.

"Like, go hunting them, and looking for their homes. And hurt or maybe kill dragons, and steal their eggs, and ruin their habitat."

I was impressed with her grasp of humans' impact on wildlife and their habitats, and I wondered how much she'd learned on her own versus what she was taught in school. Certainly, she was an insatiable reader, and smart enough to realize that dragons, like many kinds of wildlife, were endangered. Of course, the world at large had no idea that dragons existed among wild animals, and that they were in dire need of conservation.

The thought of dragons waiting just outside the clinic broke me out of my reverie. My helper, not knowing where to find supplies and equipment, mostly watched as I set up the anesthesia machine and monitors, turned on the oxygen, and drew up sedative medication in a syringe. Ember smoothed layers of towels over the treatment table as I swapped out the syringe needle for a larger, longer one.

As I capped the syringe, Ember turned to me with a hint of trepidation on her face. "Mom, do I need to hold him down when you give that?"

"No, kiddo, the mama dragon will hold him for me. Assuming she's still outside. And, I think she will be; she said she would stay."

"Oh. I hope she's still here." She looked relieved, but not entirely.

"You can stand watch at the back door when I give the injection. What did you do with the cookies, by the way?"

"I hung them on the hook by the door. They're under my coat, so they'll be safe."

I had to laugh. Leave it to my daughter to take all precautions with cookies at stake.

"All right, Ember, not every third grader gets to say this: let's go sedate a dragon."

2

A Strange Discovery

Ember took her sentry post by the back door while I approached the dragons, still in the shadows of the elms. The hatchling rested quietly on the grass with his mother watching closely. Evidently he had tired of the skirmish; he didn't protest at all as I auscultated his chest with my stethoscope, showing only mild interest in the shiny bell of the scope. His heart beat slow and steady, resonating like a mini bass drum in his small chest. His breath sounds were normal, if a bit on the quiet side. He appeared stable and healthy enough to sedate.

"Okay, Squeak, let's make you sleep for a bit." Once I tried to restrain the hatchling's hind leg for an injection, his tiredness vanished. He squirmed and flapped his wings, stubbornly pulling away from me as I attempted to hold him in place. The mother dragon promptly quashed her baby's fight by nearly flattening him to the ground with an outstretched claw. He helplessly fluttered his wing tips and twitched his tail like an angry cat.

"Geez, mama, thanks, but you're going to squash him." Indeed, it looked like the hatchling couldn't even draw a full breath. But with him subdued, now was the time to accomplish the deed. I stretched out his hindlimb, looking for the soft spot on the inside back of the thigh, where the scales thinned out. The baby fought, almost managing to wrench his leg from my grasp. His tail painfully thumped the back of my head, and his mother grabbed his tail with her teeth to prevent him from hitting me again. I wedged my knee in front of his thigh so he couldn't pull away.

There, right in between the scales.... Which was no easy task on a moving target. As I gripped his thigh with the rest of my hand, I used my thumbnail to lift the margin of a scale. I pulled the needle cap off with my teeth, then positioned the needle tip between scales, sliding it dangerously close to my thumb. No matter how practiced I was injecting dragons, it was always risky, and I'd experienced more than a few needle injuries during my career.

Finally, I injected the sedative into the baby's thigh muscle. He snorted in protest and spat a burst of flames. But thanks to his mother's restraint, all the hatchling managed to scorch was a small stripe of lawn grass.

"Okay, mama, let him breathe. The injection is done." She lifted her claw a bit but didn't let go altogether.

I sat down on the grass to wait for the sedative to take effect, shivering in the breeze. It occurred to me that I hadn't thought to grab the stretcher. The dragon was too heavy for me to comfortably carry. Looking between Ember, standing watchfully at the door, and the drowsy hatchling, I considered whether my daughter could help with one end of the stretcher. No, with an undersized assistant carrying one end, the stretcher would be more trouble than it was worth.

The hatchling fell asleep after ten or fifteen minutes. The mother dragon lifted her claw and nudged her baby curiously.

"Yes, he's asleep, and he won't wake up until I give him a different injection. I'm glad you stayed to help. Could you please carry him as far as the door?"

In response, the mother dragon lifted the hatchling in her front claws, grappling his limp body awkwardly as his head, limbs, and wings flopped. Lifting seventy pounds of dead weight was an entirely different experience than holding seventy pounds of conscious, wiggling baby. She found her grip and plodded to the clinic door behind me, the hatchling cradled in her front claws, wings and tail dangling. Ember's eyes grew wide with wonder and unease as the dragons drew closer. I stopped at the door, protectively positioning myself between my daughter and the dragons.

"All right, hand him to me, mama, and I'll take him inside. Do you still plan to wait?"

"Wait," came the gravelly reply. Most unusual, but I wasn't about to argue.

I draped the limp hatchling's head and neck over my shoulder as I struggled to get a good grip on his body. Dragons were such awkward creatures, with four limbs, wings, and a tail; appendages were everywhere. The mother dragon let go before I was quite ready, and I stumbled and swayed, finally getting a decent hold. I wrapped my arms beneath his forelimbs and wings, hugging his heavy body to mine. The short spikes along his spine dug uncomfortably into my hands. His hind limbs hung limply in front of me, and his tail drooped to the ground. His wings sagged on either side of me, painfully pinching my skin where the wing bones pressed into my upper arms. I would definitely have bruises later.

"Okay, I've got him. I'll need him inside for at least an hour… I mean, until the moon moves to about there." Lacking available hands, I surveyed the sky and then gestured with my head vaguely west from the moon's current position. The human concept of time meant nothing to dragons. "Stay put in the shadows. I'll take good care of him."

The dragon quietly snorted and flared her wings, then turned back toward the trees. Straining under the weight of the hatchling, I turned toward the door to find Ember with eyes like saucers.

Taking care not to trip over the dragon's tail, I carefully stepped through the door and down the hall. "Close the door, please. You okay?"

"Yeah, Mom, I'm okay. I've never been so close to a grown-up dragon before." Ember had closely interacted with tiny, newborn dragons on several occasions, but she had only seen adult dragons from a safe distance. She shut the door and followed me down the hall and into the treatment area, where she wrinkled her nose. "Wow, he's stinky. He smells sort of like a skunk, but burnt."

"Yes, dragons definitely have a powerful stench." I gratefully shifted my burden onto the treatment table. Despite the cold night, I was thoroughly overheated from exertion, and immediately peeled off my coat and tossed it onto a far counter. Once I turned back to the hatchling, something caught my eye.

"Huh. That's interesting."

"What, Mom? What is it?"

"Look here." I pointed. With the dragon awake and moving, and without the benefit of good lighting, I hadn't seen the distention in his neck. Now, with him recumbent and immobile, head extended, and with bright lighting, I noticed a subtle bulge in the hatchling's neck, about a third of the distance from his head to his chest. I gently palpated the swelling, then squeezed more firmly. A muted whistle sounded from deep in the dragon's throat.

"What the hell?" I repeated. Then I looked guiltily at Ember. "Don't say that at school."

"I know, Mom. I don't say a lot of what you and Dad say when I'm at school."

I wasn't sure whether to be relieved, offended, or mortified by that. Maybe all of the above.

"Did you try to eat something you shouldn't have, little guy?" I suspected the noise was coming from something the dragon swallowed, but I couldn't yet be certain.

First things first. I fastened a cuff around the hatchling's hind leg, just above the tarsus, or ankle. The cuff was attached to a handheld monitor. Another lead from the monitor ended with a small clip, which I placed on the webbing between the dragon's toes. With bandaging tape, I gently trussed the baby's small wings together to keep them out of the way.

"Job number one," I said. "This is an easy one. When this beeps, show me the display, and I'll tell you which button to push."

"Okay."

"Job number two. You've used my stethoscope before, right? Remember which way to put it in your ears?" Ember nodded and carefully positioned the earpieces. "There you go. Now hold the bell here — do you hear his heartbeat?"

Ember gently held the bell where I indicated on the broad expanse of scales over the hatchling's deep chest. Her hands looked so small and delicate compared to the dragon. "Yeah, I hear it!" Her eyes were wide in fascination.

"Okay great. You'll need to check often to make sure you can hear it, and count the beats for me. Can you do that?"

She looked worried. "His chest is so big. How do I remember where to listen?"

"Tell you what. Let's mark the spot." I plucked a wet-erase marker from a nearby cup of motley writing utensils and drew a rough circle around the stethoscope bell on the hatchling's ruby scales.

"Will that come off?"

"Yes, it's a whiteboard marker. It will come off in the rain, if not before. Besides, he's got bigger things to worry about, or he wouldn't be here."

"Okay." Ember still looked a bit dubious.

"What's the matter?"

"He's so pretty, and the marker is ugly."

"Geez, says the kid who colored on her favorite stuffed animal when she was little. Besides, I don't care how pretty he is right now, I'm more worried about what's wrong with him and how I can fix it. Got it?"

"Can I wipe off the marker later?"

I sighed. "Okay, fine… Stand right there while you're monitoring him, all right? Whatever you do, do NOT walk in front of his mouth."

"Because of the fire or because he might bite?"

"Fire. Well, both, really. He's sedated, but sometimes when they wake up, they start biting… But don't worry, I won't let him hurt you."

Now, onto the dicier part of this endeavor. Which was to say, the fiery, toothy part. I began to open the hatchling's mouth, then had second thoughts. I donned exam gloves, a surgical mask, and chemistry lab-style protective goggles, positioned the overhead lamp, then gingerly looked into the dragon's mouth and down his throat.

Even in baby dragons, the tissues of the mouth and throat appeared leathery and hardened, the teeth darkened along the sides adjacent to the palate and tongue from breathing fire. The tissues were already toughened at birth and became progressively thicker and impervious with time. Two duct openings sat deep in the throat, on either side of the laryngeal opening, and fire issued from these. Based on past necropsy studies, I knew that the flammable substance came from organs in the abdomen that connected to the throat via ducts through the chest.

Exactly what comprised the flammable gas, and how dragons ignited it into flames, were parts of dragon physiology that I still didn't understand, despite nearly twenty years of working with them. However it worked, there was no question that fire spewed from those two ducts. I'd scorched various parts of my face more than once while rediscovering that bit of knowledge.

Delicately, I retracted the epiglottis away from the larynx using the rounded blade of a laryngoscope, taking care not to touch the fire ducts. In the past, I'd discovered the hard way that flames could sometimes be stimulated by touching the ducts or surrounding tissue. Using the lighted laryngoscope to examine deeper down the airway, I found nothing amiss, but I was also nowhere near the bulge in the dragon's neck.

Closing the dragon's mouth, I set the laryngoscope aside and sat back on my stool. I rolled the stool out of the "strike zone," pushed the goggles onto the top of my head, and stared into space for several moments as I considered my next step. I gazed vaguely toward the hatchling's bright red body, and the reflection from his scales flickered in my unfocused stare, like bits of quartz twinkling in a misty cave. He and his mother were both strikingly beautiful creatures.

"Mom, what's the matter?"

My focus snapped away from the dragon's scales and onto my daughter's face instead. "I'm thinking. Heart beating okay? And everything look okay on the monitor?"

"Nothing is blinking or beeping. And his heart rate is twenty beats per minute."

"Wait, how did you learn to count beats per minute? I didn't teach you that, did I?"

"Jess taught me."

"Oh. That's cool. Good job," I added distractedly, as I resumed my contemplation.

"What are you going to do, Mom?"

"I'm figuring that out. I'm just thinking through how I'm going to make it work." What I really wanted was to x-ray the dragon's neck. And under normal circumstances — if one could ever consider veterinary medicine for dragons normal — I'd have done it. The hatchling was small enough to radiograph using my standard x-ray table, although it wouldn't be much fun to wrestle the heavy, sedated dragon into radiology. My concern had nothing to do with his size, but with the effect of radiation on a dragon's camouflage systems. Upon exposure to focused radiation, as with an x-ray beam, dragon tissues glowed. Some component in their scales was stimulated to fluoresce by the radiation, I was certain, but I didn't know exactly what. The effect was temporary, hours at most, but it wrecked their ability to hide during that time. Even with their camouflage systems in full force, the glowing body parts were a dead giveaway.

For once, rather than dumping a sick hatchling on me and immediately leaving, the mother had stayed, waiting for her baby. Ironically, this was the one time I wished she'd flown off, so I could x-ray the hatchling and then kennel him overnight to allow the glow to dissipate. Well, I wasn't going to send her off now for fear she might not come back for days, and I wasn't going to release a glowing dragon into the night sky. Despite dragons' talents at hiding, any added length of time the mother lurked outside the clinic increased her risk of discovery and conflict with humans, so I wanted to send both dragons away as soon as possible. I'd have to make do without x-rays.

"Mom, his heart speed — I mean heart rate — is sixteen. Is that okay?"

"Sixteen beats per minute?"

"Yeah, sixteen. It sounds really slow."

"Show me the monitor. Okay, see those numbers?" I pointed without touching the monitor with my dragon saliva-slicked glove, and my daughter nodded, brow creased in concentration. "Those are his blood pressures, and they look great. The first number, where it says 108 — now 110 — is what's called the systolic pressure. If that number drops below one hundred, you need to tell me. And it should beep if that happens. Can you watch and listen for that?"

Ember nodded confidently. "Yes, Mom."

"You've seen anesthetized dogs and cats, and their heart rates are much higher. Dragons' heart rates sometimes drop really low, but that's because they are large and athletic, and their hearts are big and powerful. Does that make sense?"

"Yeah, kind of. His sitsolic — is that how you say it? — is 112."

"Systolic, and you're doing a great job monitoring him."

Ember's furrowed brow lifted in excitement. "Can I work for you when I'm older?"

"Sure, if you want to."

"Would I get to work with dragons?"

"Well, if you want to work with dragons, you have to learn how to be as safe as possible around them. Not all my staff like to work with dragons, because they can be dangerous. Especially the adults. So, they don't have to help with the dragons if they're not comfortable."

"Jess likes them."

"Jess loves them. In fact, Jess is the only person I've ever known who wasn't frightened of the dragons when she met them."

"Was I scared the first time I met a dragon?"

"Well, no, you were fascinated. But then, you were a baby, and so was the dragon. It's different when you grow up around dragons."

Now I needed to figure out my end of things. The hatchling had shown no signs of respiratory distress, no obstructive breathing, no pale or bluish mucous membranes (such that could be judged in species with thickened, leathery tissues), no increased respiratory rate or effort, and his lungs sounded fine. This could not be an airway issue. The swelling or distention had to have been in the esophagus or the soft tissues of the neck, and I strongly suspected this was an esophageal issue. My heart sank. Owing to the inaccessibility of the esophagus, diagnosing and resolving the problem would be difficult.

"Ember, watch him closely. I'm going to set up the endoscope."

"What's that?"

"It's a video camera, but for your insides." Truth be told, I wasn't very proficient with endoscopy. We'd bought the scope for my partner, Dr. Beth, who had far more training in endoscopy than I did. But I knew how to set it up, or at least I was pretty sure I remembered, and I'd done some simple things with endoscopy in the past. I was hoping this would turn out to be easier than I feared.

Fumbling the cables, I connected the power supply, camera, and scope to the base unit, then the video cable to the monitor. Then I turned the power on and fiddled with the settings while I held the scope to my hand, trying to project a recognizable image of my palm on the screen.

"Do you know what you're doing with that?"

"Shush. No, I'm just making this up as I go."

Ember smirked, but I was only half kidding. "Will he wake up before you're done with him?"

"No, dexmedetomidine lasts a long time in dragons. If he starts getting light, there's another medication that I'll give him to keep him asleep. Sometimes I have to give propofol just to get them sedate enough. But this guy is doing nicely on the first injection alone."

"Oh. Aren't they usually hooked to that machine?" She pointed.

"Smart girl. You're referring to the anesthesia machine, and you're right, dogs and cats are usually hooked up to that. And they have a tube down their windpipe, or at least an oxygen mask over their nose. But I don't do that with dragons unless I have to. Any guesses why?"

She shook her head. "No, why?"

"Because oxygen is flammable, and what do dragons breathe?"

"OH." Her eyes were once again as wide as saucers.

"Don't worry. I'm going to put a tube in this little guy to control his airway, because I need to put the scope down his esophagus. He probably won't need oxygen, but if he does, it can still be done safely; it just takes a lot of care. I won't let an explosion happen."

Ember stared intently at the hatchling's head, her eyes wide with concern. With good reason — dragons were far more challenging and dangerous patients than dogs and cats. Although, any animal could be dangerous; I'd probably been injured as many times by domestic cats as I had been by dragons. Cat bites weren't the same as dragon burns, but cats had put me in the hospital more than once. Dragons had never done that — yet.

Ready with the endotracheal tube, I pushed the goggles back over my eyes, and carefully opened the hatchling's mouth. I propped his jaws apart using a section of old tubing between his teeth, and delicately inserted the endotracheal tube down the dragon's airway. The tube slid neatly into place down the windpipe, and foul-smelling dragon breath swooshed through the tube, fogging my goggles. No flames appeared, and I exhaled in relief. I tied the tube in place, the end sticking out just past the hatchling's muzzle, then inflated the cuff that ballooned inside the airway, anchoring the tube in place.

Then, I donned a silicone grill mitt over one hand. I'd soaked a small huck towel in tap water and clamped long forceps to it. With the heavy glove, I awkwardly palmed the forceps and guided the towel into the dragon's throat, packing the toweling over the fire ducts. I exhaled again, only then realizing that I had been holding my breath. I pulled the silicone glove off. The mitt protected my hand from flame emissions effectively, but made it difficult to handle anything that required dexterity. I'd have to find something that worked better in the future. But that was the reality of dragon medicine: an endless search for different and better ways to do things, since no textbook existed to guide me.

Now for the endoscope. Again, using the laryngoscope, I slowly slid the scope into the dragon's throat to the side of the endotracheal tube. I pushed the toweling aside just a bit, and guided the scope down the dragon's esophagus, carefully avoiding the fire ducts. Using forceps, I tucked the soaked toweling snugly around the endoscope. Now that the scope was in place, I rested the dragon's head on the treatment table, and shook my left hand, which ached from holding the dragon's jaw and the laryngoscope at the same time.

"Hey, Mom," Ember whispered tentatively. "Can I ask a question?"

I realized she'd been waiting for a break in the action to speak. "You just did, but yes, ask another one."

"Why did you stuff a wet rag in his throat?"

"It's not a rag, it's a huck towel. A surgical towel. You know, like the ones we use for draping in surgery." My surgical suite had a big window to the hallway, and on many occasions, Ember had perched on a stool, watching me perform surgery through the window.

"Oh. But why did you put one in his throat?"

"That covers the fire ducts. So, if he accidentally breathes fire, the flames will hit the wet towel. It might scorch the towel, but I'd rather ruin a huck towel than get my face burned. And I'm wearing goggles, too, just in case."

"Oh. That's smart."

"Well, I learned the hard way."

"I remember when you came home with your eyebrows burned."

I sighed. "Which time?" My assistant giggled.

Watching the monitor as the normal pink tissue slid by, I

guided the scope down the dragon's esophagus. My goggles were beginning to fog, and I paused to push them to the top of my head. Just as I pushed the scope a bit further, I encountered the source of the problem. Something unquestionably foreign entered the field of view: a plasticky, rounded object with a perfect hole in the center. The thing was a garish shade of pinkish-purple under the light of the endoscope, and the surface reflected harshly through the video feed, irritating my eyes as it flashed across the monitor. I paused and tried to get my bearings as I frowned at the screen.

"What the hell is that?"

"It's okay, Mom, I won't repeat that at school," Ember teased.

I shot her a rueful glance. "Okay, great... What does this look like to you?" I tilted the monitor her direction.

"It's... some kind of toy? Like a dog toy! Is that a squeaker hole?"

"Oh! You might be right." Trust my kid to recognize a dog toy, if that was indeed what it was. We'd find out once I got it out. But how to accomplish that...?

"He swallowed a dog toy?" Ember asked.

"Whatever it is, he tried to. He didn't succeed, or it wouldn't be stuck in his esophagus."

"What if he'd swallowed it all the way?"

"Then it would get stuck in his intestines." Which raised a good point. I couldn't just push it down into his stomach, or he'd end up with a worse problem once intestinal obstruction developed. "You know, he's lucky that you talked me into picking up the cookies tonight. If we hadn't, he wouldn't have been able to eat until someone came along, maybe not until Monday. He probably would have been very sick by then."

"I'm glad we came for the cookies, Mom."

"Yeah, me too, kiddo. Thanks for helping me with this little guy. Speaking of which, what's his blood pressure?"

"It's 118. And I just counted his heart rate, and it's twenty."

"Perfect. You're doing a great job."

Ember beamed with pride. "Thanks, Mom."

Positioning the scope in front of the squeaker hole, I tentatively pressed on the bulge in the dragon's neck. Sure enough, the object shifted on the monitor as the toy compressed, and a distinct *squeak* emanated up the esophagus. Then the object resumed its original position as it re-inflated itself. I smiled, and Ember snickered. Her identification of the object as a dog toy was probably accurate. Such a strange case, this was. On a regular basis, I performed surgery to remove various objects from the gastrointestinal tracts of dogs and cats: rocks, socks, hair ties, holiday ornaments, and yes, toys. But I had never met a dragon that swallowed a toy, let alone one that squeaked when he swallowed. I laughed at the absurdity.

"Can I squeeze it?"

"Sure, but be gentle — once! Okay, that's enough."

My assistant snickered again.

I wasn't yet sure how I'd grab hold of the object, but it would be easier to manipulate deflated. Asking Ember to continue her monitoring, I fetched a second large, rigid endotracheal tube, a scalpel blade, a blade handle, and some stiff wire. My daughter watched curiously as I anchored the wire around the blade handle, twisting it to secure the handle in place, then twisted the wire into a long tail. Then I snapped the blade onto the scalpel handle.

"Are you making a spear?"

"Something like that. Or like a really long X-Acto knife."

I measured the endotracheal tube against my crude extended

blade and marked the wire where the tube ended. Then, I slid the tube into the dragon's throat, attempting to guide it down the esophagus. Between the original endotracheal tube in the dragon's windpipe and the second tube in the esophagus, it was a tight fit, and I worried about how much pressure I might put on the fire ducts.

"I wonder…"

"Wonder what?"

"Whether I can fit the endoscope through the tube." As I gently pushed, the scope slid neatly through the endotracheal tube. "Yes, look at that. It fits."

"Are you really making this up as you go?"

"Pretty much. Veterinary medicine is all about adapting things to all different kinds of species and problems. More so when the species aren't supposed to exist. Okay, here we go…."

I positioned the tube right over the object, then carefully withdrew the endoscope. Then, I delicately slid the scalpel blade with its extended wire shaft down the tube. The fit was tight, but it worked. When the marked portion of the wire reached the end of the tube, I stopped advancing it. "Okay, ready for this?"

"Are you going to pop it?"

"Yes, that's the idea." I advanced the scalpel forward, past the end of the tube in the esophagus, into the object. No *pop*, but the bulge in the dragon's neck visibly moved several centimeters toward his stomach.

"It moves that easily? How on earth did it not go all the way to this stomach when he swallowed it, or at least to the esophageal valve?" I muttered, shaking my head. "So weird. Here, Ember, I want your hand to keep that thing from sliding farther down the esophagus. Hold right here and press firmly."

She did as instructed. "You're not going to stab me, are you?"

"No, just keep holding until I say so." Advancing the tube, I felt it come to a stop on the toy, now held in place by Ember's hand. Pushing the blade once again, I heard a sharp *pop*, followed by a short swish of air. The distention in the dragon's neck shrank a bit. "Now press on his neck, over the toy." After a lot of pressure, the bulge reduced only a small amount, and the squeaker still made an audible noise.

"I think it needs a larger hole. Or more holes. Hang on, hold still for a moment." I advanced the blade again into the plastic item, then again, and again. Air hissed, the squeaker was silent, and the bump in the dragon's neck deflated to a fraction of its former size.

"Shoot, I should have tried to push it toward his mouth while it was still inflated. I didn't realize it would move that easily until I tried to stab it. Let's see if it will move now…" I attempted to manipulate the deflated object up the esophagus using pressure on the dragon's neck. "Nope, it won't budge."

"So how are you going to get it out?" Ember asked.

Sighing, I closed my eyes and rubbed my arm over my forehead, which was slick with sweat. "I'm not yet sure, kiddo. I'll figure it out."

The object had to come out that night. If I failed to remove it through his throat, the only other option was to push it into his stomach and do abdominal surgery. However, I couldn't do that without a trained technician, and none of my staff were available. If I didn't succeed, the hatchling wouldn't be able to eat. He would rapidly get sick, and maybe even die. Ember would be crushed, and honestly, I'd have trouble forgiving myself. But removing the toy would be a tough and time-consuming challenge.

This was turning into far more of an ordeal than I'd hoped for.

3

A Slippery Challenge

Perusing the endoscopy instruments on the rack, I couldn't find anything that would grip the rubbery material well enough to extract the object from the dragon's esophagus. The tiny tools we used for grasping tissues and obtaining biopsies were far too small for a toy. Finally, I selected the loop tool. Perhaps I could lasso part of the deflated rubber and cinch it tight enough to pull it out. It didn't seem promising, but I had to try something.

With the tube out of the dragon's esophagus, I repositioned the endoscope and advanced it until I could see the object, which now looked much flatter, with several slashes from the scalpel. Two of the cuts had intersected to form a V, and the rubber stuck out like an arrow.

"Okay, Ember, hold your hand behind the toy. Don't let it move."

For twenty frustrating minutes, I tried to slide the loop over some portion of the object: first one fold, then another, then the V-shaped protrusion. Finally — finally! – the loop caught. I froze, then slowly, carefully, cinched the loop down until I could secure the material against the end of the scope.

"Mom, you're not breathing."

"Okay, you're right, I am now… Let go of his neck. I don't want any pressure that might keep that thing from moving. Now, let's see if this holds, or if it just rips off. I don't think the part I've got hold of is very sturdy."

Tentatively, I began to withdraw the scope, and the object moved with it. Despite some resistance, I pulled it up and up, closer and closer to hatchling's throat. The screen showed the loop still attached to the object, but it looked like the material might be starting to tear.

Please hold, please hold....

As the object reached the dragon's throat, I ducked my head to the side and continued to pull, knowing I would put pressure over the fire ducts. But as I pulled harder against the increased resistance of the throat, the sliver of material cinched to the endoscope tore off, and I was abruptly left holding the liberated endoscope, with a piece of slimy, glittery, lavender vinyl attached to its tip.

"Glitter—that's why it's so reflective in the scope," I mused.

"Mom, it tore off, didn't it? What now?"

"It's almost out. I can reach it with forceps now. Here, hold your hand right there. Now you'll keep it from moving back into the esophagus while I grab it."

Pushing the toweling and leathery tissue out of the way with the laryngoscope, I spied the lavender surface of the object. I inserted the tips of long forceps into the dragon's throat, clamped them over a fold in the vinyl, and began to pull.

"Mom! Your goggles—"

Too late. As I yanked the toy free from the dragon's throat, flames spurted over my hand and into my unprotected face.

"Dammit!" I cried, flinching and dropping the forceps and the dragon's head, his jaw thumping onto the treatment table. Yanking off my smoldering mask, I tossed it into the sink, where it fizzled out.

My exam glove was in tatters, but it had protected my hand from worse burns. I peeled off what was left of the blue nitrile to examine the skin. Red splotches marred my fingers, but they weren't seriously wounded.

"Okay, what does my face look like?"

Ember's face was inscrutable as she carefully looked me over. "One eyebrow is kind of missing, and the other one has little curled hairs. And there are some curled hairs in your bangs, too. Like a slinky."

"Yeah, that's what hair looks like when it's singed. Is my face red? Are there blisters?" My face stung but wasn't painful, so I didn't think I had incurred any major damage.

"Your forehead is sort of red. I don't see any blisters. Mom?"

"Yes, Ember?"

"Can I laugh? Because I kind of want to."

Sighing, I couldn't help but smile. "Fine, knock yourself out. I made a stupid mistake, and I'm lucky I didn't get hurt. Just singed. Go ahead and laugh."

My assistant giggled at my expense while I retrieved the toy I'd flung onto the floor, still clamped to the forceps. I held them up, turning the slimy, deflated object over in the light.

"Look at that," I said. "I've never seen a squeaky ball for dogs that's glittery."

"I've seen one just like that!" Ember exclaimed. "My friend Corrina has one for her dog. Except hers is blue, not purple."

"Well, tell her not to let a dragon take it. My guess is a dragon found this in someone's yard and took it for their hoard. Or maybe a dog lost it while they were out on a walk. Either way, Squeak" — I gestured to the unconscious hatchling — "or his mom picked it up and kept it. And then Squeak tried to eat it."

"That wasn't very smart."

"No, it wasn't. Let's wake him up and send him home." Gingerly, I deflated and removed the endotracheal tube from the dragon's windpipe, then the sodden, scorched huck towel. This time, my goggles were firmly in place. No flames emerged.

"Where does he live?"

"Probably somewhere in the mountains," I replied as I reached for the sedative reversal medication and a syringe. Our valley was surrounded by rugged hills and mountains with ample hiding spots for wildlife. "I have a pretty good idea of where some of them live, but I've never been to a dragon's home."

"Would you? Visit a dragon's home, I mean?"

"If the dragon knew I was there and didn't mind, I would take a look out of curiosity. But if I hadn't met the dragon, it would be dangerous to walk in unannounced, not to mention rude. I found a dragon's hoard once, so I'm certain I was close to their home. But I didn't know where the dragon was, and I definitely didn't want he or she to think I was stealing something. I left immediately."

"Do you think every dragon has a treasure hoard?"

"Probably not." I inserted the syringe needle between the scales of the hatchling's thigh, the opposite leg this time, and injected the anesthetic reversal agent into the muscle. "Some dragons are interested in hoarding, but not that many. And 'treasure' depends on your definition of the word. Dragons that hoard may have some valuable things like coins and gemstones, but they also tend to collect things that we don't think of as treasure. Like pretty rocks, and shiny bits of junk metal, and sparkly plastic things."

"And purple squeaky balls."

"Yes, apparently squeaky toys, too."

I helped Ember disconnect and shut down the monitor, then spread a blanket on the floor adjacent to the treatment table. I wrestled the heavy hatchling onto it and peeled the tape away from his wings as my assistant dutifully scrubbed the marker lines from his chest. He started to come around as Ember rubbed the wet towel over his scales, twitching and lifting his head and wings.

"All right, we're going to use the blanket to drag Squeak down the hall to his mama. Can you help with one end? No, the other end. I'll take the fiery side."

Together, we pushed and pulled the hatchling across the floor, through the treatment room door, and down the hallway, using the blanket as a floppy stretcher. The baby awakened more and more as we went, looking around with bewilderment.

"Let's stop here until he's more awake. Then we'll let him be with his mom."

Placing my hand over the dragon's shoulders, I sat down on the floor next to the hatchling, safely out of the "strike zone." I leaned back against the wall, watching the baby closely as he wobbled from the sedative.

"What's his mom's name?" Ember asked.

"I don't know. What do you think it should be?"

Ember furrowed her brow in thought for a moment. "Scarlet," she announced.

"Scarlet," I mused. "Scarlet and Squeak. I like it."

Ember spied her coat on the rack by the back door, with the coveted bag of cookies tucked safely behind it. "Mom, while we're waiting, can I have a cookie?"

"It's 'may I,' not 'can I.' That's getting to be a bad habit. But, yes, you were a great help, you've definitely earned a cookie. Go ahead."

"Yay!" Rustling of plastic immediately commenced, quickly followed by the sounds of happy munching. The dragon took interest and stumbled in her direction, still shaky but gaining some coordination.

"Ember, you should go to the office to eat, he's way too fascinated with—"

"Look, Mom, Squeak wants a cookie."

"No, he does not need a—"

The dragon abruptly jerked his head and neck forward as he snatched a cookie from my daughter's outstretched hand. He gulped it down as multicolored cookie sprinkles scattered in all directions.

"EMBER RAYNE, YOU DID NOT JUST FEED A COOKIE TO THE DRAGON!"

My daughter shot a devilish grin my direction. "He likes it!"

The hatchling swayed precariously, nearly falling over as he eagerly reached for more. A bit of yellow frosting adorned his nose.

"No, NO MORE! Take the cookies out," I scolded as I scrambled to my feet to shoo Ember and the hatchling away from each other. "Dragons are obligate carnivores; cookies aren't good for them."

"Neither are squeaky balls, but he ate that," Ember retorted.

"Yeah, and look what happened? He had to come see the vet. Off with you now! Take the cookies to the office. And that's enough for you, too. Save some for tomorrow."

A giggle floated down the hallway as my impish child made her escape. I sighed. And I'd thought baby dragons were mischievous. My kid had them beat. In truth, the cookie probably wouldn't do any harm, but I didn't want her in the habit of feeding human foods to any animals, including dragons.

The hatchling was now solidly on his feet, flapping his wings without wavering as much. I thought he was fine to go home, as long as his mother didn't allow him to fly until the sedative completely wore off. Although, I hadn't thought to verify that his mother was still waiting for him.

"You'd better still be here," I muttered as I opened the door. Thankfully, she was lying in the shadows beneath the trees. I could barely make out her shape, recumbent on the grass next to a gigantic pine. Not wanting to yell, I walked across the parking lot to talk to her.

"Your son tried to swallow a dog's toy, and it got stuck. I don't know whether it came from his hoard, yours, or someone else's, but please watch and make sure he doesn't swallow any other inanimate objects. You may take him home, but he's still unsteady from sedation, so don't allow him to fly until…" I glanced skyward. "Until the moon and stars are in the same position after one sun. Does that make sense?"

The dragon snorted, which I took as an affirmative.

"Oh, and I don't know how long he went without food with that thing stuck in his throat, but he's definitely hungry. The sedation doesn't seem to have dampened his appetite at all. He already ate a cookie that my daughter fed him."

The dragon tilted her head and looked at me quizzically.

My eyes flitted guiltily to the side, then back to the dragon. "Sorry. That wasn't supposed to happen, but I'm sure he'll be fine." I wasn't sure if dragons even knew what cookies were, but I wasn't about to attempt explaining.

The mother dragon followed me to the back door of the clinic.

Opening the door, I found the hatchling had abandoned his blanket, and was wandering uncertainly down the hallway, no doubt following the scent of Ember's cookies.

"Hey, get back here, Squeak. Your mom is here."

The mother squeezed her great head and neck through the back door, reaching with one large claw to grasp the baby's tail as I jumped aside. Her horns and spikes scraped noisily against the heavy metal door and its frame, scratching long lines into the many layers of paint. She pulled the little dragon backward as he squawked and struggled in protest, then grabbed him around his chest and wrestled him out the back door. At least the squawk was a normal, indignant hatchling noise, unlike the unnatural squeak with which he'd arrived.

"Okay, then. That was a bit rougher than necessary." Glancing nervously at the nearby homes, thankfully I saw no faces in window frames. Amazing, how much noise the clinic's neighbors were willing to ignore.

As the dragon carried her still-squawking hatchling across the parking lot, I called down the hall to my daughter. "Ember, do you want to watch them take flight? Hurry!"

Small footsteps pattered as Ember sprinted down the hall and materialized at my side, panting. "I saw Scarlet grab him," she said. "I think she was kind of mean."

"Well, dragon babies are tough. I don't think he minds so much. Did you see how mean he was being to his mom earlier before we sedated him? I think he'll be just fine."

Gravel skittered and cold air whooshed across the parking lot as the dragon lifted off, the stubborn hatchling clutched firmly in her front claws. Light from the streetlamp glimmered on crimson scales for a fleeting moment, quickly fading as the dragons' camouflage mechanisms set in. The clouds subtly rippled as the mother and baby disappeared into their depths. Then, nothing.

"I can't see them anymore. They disappeared so quick," Ember whispered in awe.

"Yes, their camouflage skills are incredible."

"Mom?"

"Yes?"

"Can I — *may* I — call Dad to tell him about the dragons?"

Looking at my watch, I shook my head. "Absolutely not, not tonight. He's in a different time zone, and we'd wake him up. Also, it's way past your bedtime."

"Okay," she replied dejectedly.

"You may call him tomorrow. And he'll be home the next day. Now, let's clean up and go home."

As we tidied up the treatment area, Ember spied the forceps firmly clamped around the squeaky toy. She gingerly picked them up. "Mom, they left the ball behind. Don't you think they'll want it back?"

"Don't touch the ball. Dragon saliva will make your skin itch. And I doubt they want it. If the mother wanted it, believe me, she would have made that clear. Squeak probably doesn't remember it."

"Can I have it?"

"Ember… why, just *why*, would you want a slimy punctured squeaky ball that's been in a dragon's esophagus?"

"Because it's cool."

"It's disgusting!"

"But it's like a souvenir! And it won't take up much room."

Sighing, I relented. "All right, fine, but wash it off first."

My helper scrubbed off her slimy prize while I wiped down the treatment table and put away supplies. Finally, close to three hours after we'd gone to the clinic "just real fast" for cookies, we made it home. While Ember was exuberant from her unexpected dragon adventure, I was exhausted.

42

4

An Odd Exchange

Two days later, my husband returned from his trip, and our daughter excitedly regaled him with the tale of our escapade. She proudly presented the saggy, formerly-squeaky ball to him. He was both impressed and horrified.

"You *kept* it? That's... kind of gross. But, I'm glad you got to help your mom. I think." Jon had never been entirely comfortable around the dragons, and he wasn't thrilled about Ember interacting with them. His sideways glance to me made it clear that I would get an earful later.

Days passed, and the squeaky toy lost its novel appeal. I found my daughter planting the ball, impaled on a stick, in a flower bed in our back yard.

"Ember, what are you doing?"

"I'm going to see if Scarlet and Squeak come back for it."

"You're leaving it there? Kiddo, I doubt that the dragons will look for it here. They left the ball at the clinic, after all."

"But, Mom, I've seen dragons in our back yard before. Several times."

"Well, yes, but if you lost a toy at a restaurant, would you go looking for it at the chef's house? I think not."

The glittery ball remained planted on its stick for over a week, and Ember faithfully checked it every day. I expected it would soon be buried in snow and forgotten over the winter, only to emerge in the spring as a soggy memento of our exploits. However, I was wrong.

Late on a Saturday night, two weeks after the squeaky hatchling's ordeal, I slipped into the back yard with the compost pail in hand. As I rounded the walkway near the flower bed, I saw a flash of crimson out of the corner of my eye and froze, staring into the darkness and waiting for the flash to reappear.

No further sight nor sound occurred, and I began to think I'd imagined the vision of red. After years of seeing dragons in strange places, my mind sometimes played tricks on me and found dragons where none existed. While dragons certainly visited me at home, that was only when they needed medical care. They would have wanted to get my attention and keep it. Whatever I'd seen, if anything, hadn't stayed around.

Slowly, I set down the pail with a quiet *clink* on the stone pathway and crept closer to the flower bed. Ember's stick was still in place, shrouded in shadows. I couldn't make out the squeaky toy, but it was also dark, and for all I could tell, the ball might be hiding in the tangle of dead and dying plant material below.

Squinting out into the ravine behind the yard, I tried to make out anything resembling a dragon. It was so impossibly dark, an entire family of dragons could have been lurking there and I wouldn't know it, even with my practiced eye. With a shrug, I emptied the compost, went back inside, and went to bed.

By the following morning, I'd nearly forgotten about Ember's squeaky ball and its possible disappearance. As I dumped vegetable peelings into the metal pail, I thought back to my strange vision during my walk to the compost pile the night before.

"Ember, I almost forgot. You should check the flower bed today. I think you might see something interesting." Ember gasped in excitement and jumped up. "And remember to wear a coat… and shoes!" I added, as she dashed for the door in her socks.

She ran out the door with her shoes half on, her unzipped coat flapping in her wake. Moments later, I heard an excited shout, and she dashed back inside, yelling all the way: "MOM MOM MOM! LOOK!"

She thrust her small hand in front of my face and unclenched her fist. Resting on her palm was an irregular chunk of shiny, yellow, metallic material, about the size of a flattened walnut. *It looks like… could it be? Surely it can't be…*

"Is that gold?" I whispered, as I picked up the heavy lump in my fingers and turned it over in my hand. I'd seen small bits of gold before that our friends had panned below some of Idaho's old gold mines, and the nugget definitely resembled those. But this was larger than anything our friends had ever found. "Ember, where did you find this?"

"Right by the stick! The ball is gone, and Mom, I think they left that for me!"

"Like, a trade? An exchange? Wow, I've never seen such a thing. Dragons have given me gifts before, but nothing as valuable as a gold nugget. I wonder how much it's worth?" I mused.

"Whoa, what is that?" My husband had emerged from the study to see what the fuss was about. "Is that *gold*? That looks like gold! Where…? how…?"

"Ember found this in the flower bed. We think the dragons left it."

"The *dragons*?" He frowned in disbelief.

"May I take it to school?" Ember pleaded. "I want to show my friends!"

"No! Definitely not. Ember, if this is real gold, it's worth a lot of money. Let's weigh it on the gram scale and see…"

The three of us crowded around the kitchen scale and stared at the digital display as Ember carefully placed the nugget on the tray. The numbers flickered, then settled.

"Almost a half-ounce," Jon announced. "That has to be worth several hundred dollars! Why couldn't the dragons have brought this kind of stuff during the recession, when the clinic nearly went under?" My husband had once been our office manager, and he did not approve of the veterinary care I provided for the dragons, in large part because of the costs of supplies, medications, and food.

I laughed. "Apparently, to them the squeaky ball is more valuable than gold. If I asked for payment, they would probably bring shiny plastic party favors."

"So what are you going to do with it?" Jon asked.

The three of us exchanged glances. First, of course, we would need to verify that the nugget was actually gold. If it was, there were so many possibilities. We could sell it to pay bills (of which we had many), squirrel it away for a rainy day, or make it into something: jewelry or maybe a figurine.

"Hey, doesn't your jeweler friend owe you a favor?" Jon asked me.

"Yes, she says she does. For taking care of her dogs on Christmas." I stared at my husband, an idea taking shape. "Are you thinking what I'm thinking?"

We set about brainstorming a pendant design in the form of the creatures that were such a large and unique part of my career. The dragons had become inextricably woven through the story of not just my life, but my family's lives too. It seemed only fitting that their gift of gold, which the dragons evidently considered to be as valuable as a beloved glittery squeaky ball, should be made into their image.

I visited my jeweler "friend," if one could call her that, since I only ever saw her in my clinic or in her shop.

"Well, I'll tell you what," she informed me, examining the gold nugget through a jeweler's loupe. "Usually we charge five hundred for this type of work."

Wincing, I wondered if this wasn't such a great idea after all.

"But," she continued, "how about the next time my dogs are sick, you discount their bill, and we'll call it even?"

I thought it over. The jeweler had a bad habit of feeding her Yorkshire terriers generous portions of holiday dinners. Inevitably, her dogs would get sick on Thanksgiving or Christmas. Either way, she would undoubtedly cash in on the trade agreement soon.

"Sure," I nodded. "I'll be around over the holidays."

The jeweler laughed. "Whatever makes you think it would be a holiday?"

I gritted my teeth to avoid retorting that at least one of her dogs had been sick for every major holiday, without fail, for the past three years. "No idea," I fibbed.

A few weeks passed. Life and work went on as usual. I further honed my skills with a brow pencil while my missing eyebrow grew back. My days at the clinic were filled with treating "normal" patients, and many of my evenings were devoted to managing whatever sick or injured dragons came along. There were always new cases and challenges ahead, and the only thing I knew to expect was the unexpected.

Jon spent his workdays staring at computers, which he found much less stressful than dragons. (Personally, I'd have happily taken the dragons over spreadsheets any day.) As November gave way to December, Jon and Ember put up holiday decorations. I came home from work to find a miniature plastic dragon skeleton, a holdover from Halloween, on the front step. He jauntily sported a Santa hat and held a strand of twinkling holiday lights in his mouth.

Ember gave her dad an unpleasant holiday gift one morning in form of an announcement: "When I grow up, I want to be a veterinarian. And I want to be a dragon specialist!"

Jon was horrified. I was thrilled and flattered that she wanted to follow in my footsteps, though I didn't have the heart to tell her there was no such thing as board certification for dragon medicine.

Mid-December, the jeweler called to tell me the pendant was ready. There was even a bit of gold left over, which I sold. The proceeds, enough to pay for food and medication for several hatchlings, went to the clinic's trust fund.

Ember became the proud and reverent owner of the solid gold dragon pendant. It would always be available to sell if she needed, but I truly hoped she'd keep it. For now, it hung on her wall: a majestic mother dragon nuzzling her tiny hatchling, both framed by an intricately scrolled golden hoop. The pendant glinted in the soft glow of Ember's bedside lamp, an enduring reminder of the evening we had gone to the clinic for cookies and teamed up to help a rather unusual patient.

Ember would tell the story to her children and grandchildren, and perhaps even pass on the pendant to them. But no matter what, she would always keep the memory of helping me remove the squeaky hatchling's squeaker, quite possibly saving his life.

* * *

To Be Continued

Epilogue

The jeweler's Yorkies quickly took advantage of our trade agreement, with two out of three requiring hospitalization for pancreatitis the day following Christmas. The culprit? Ham from Christmas dinner. Evidently, dragons weren't the only creatures eating things they shouldn't.

* * *

Acknowledgement

I owe heartfelt thanks to a great many people; more than I can reasonably list here, but I'll offer a subset.

To the Dragon Doc Tales editing, web design, graphic design, and illustration team: Sofia, Stacey, Elena, Nick, and J. You are all so creative and talented, and a joy to work with. Thank you for your skills, hard work, and encouragement.

To my family and friends, who are my biggest fans and most ardent supporters: Joshua, J, Marilynn, NJ, Lucia, Theresa, Greg, Dina, Mark, and Angel. Thank you for tolerating my frenzied writing jags and endless pleas for suggestions and opinions.

Thank you, David, for fielding my texts about the finer points of grammar and punctuation. You are an invaluable resource.

To my colleagues and coworkers in veterinary medicine, including the Alta team and the Moms with DVMs group (several of whom are my beta readers): you are all amazing. Never forget it. Thank you for your feedback and cheerleading.

Especially to J: you will forever be my heart walking around outside my body. I am so proud of you, and I love you so much. Thank you for being you.

About the Author

On a summer day long ago, Dr. S. K. Burkman climbed a mountain, got sick, and hallucinated a dragon. Thus began a lifelong fascination with dragons, and many exhaustion-fueled musings on what they might be like as patients.

Originally from Colorado and British Columbia, Dr. Burkman earned her doctorate in veterinary medicine at Colorado State University. As a busy veterinarian, Dr. Burkman keeps her sanity by writing about dragons. Many of her own adventures and misadventures are woven into her novels.

Outside of work and writing, she enjoys hiking, backpacking, kayaking, travel, cake baking and decorating, and looking for dragons. She has been married to Joshua for over twenty years, and they have one child. Dr. Burkman and her family reside in Idaho with their motley assortment of pets, and maybe, just maybe, a dragon or two.

You can connect with me on:

- https://thedragondoc.com
- http://twitter.com/iamthedragondoc
- http://facebook.com/iamthedragondoc
- https://www.amazon.com/author/dr.s.k.burkman
- https://www.goodreads.com/author/show/23050141.Dr_S_K_Burkman

Subscribe to my newsletter:

- https://thedragondoc.com

Also by Dr. S. K. Burkman

Now that you are acquainted with The Dragon Doc and her rather unusual patients in *Squeaky Hatchling*, find out where it all began in *Wings and Wounds*. Published in 2022, *Wings and Wounds* is Dr. Burkman's first full-length novel and the prequel to *Squeaky Hatchling*. Additional sequels are to follow, as well as *Common Disorders of Dragons*, a veterinary textbook on dragon medicine.

"The Dragon Doc's Wings and Wounds *takes the reader on a fantastical journey through the trials and tribulations of veterinary medicine for the most magnificent of beasts. Dr. S. K. Burkman wields a fiery sense of humor that leaves the reader in stitches while also tugging at the heartstrings. Be prepared for a wild flight... and don't forget to pack the burn salve."*
  - N.J. Gallegos, Author of *The Broken Heart*

"Fascinating insight into the veterinary care of dragons! Very well-written and captivating book - couldn't put it down."
  - D.H.

"I'm not convinced that this author doesn't actually treat dragons! I started this fun book not certain of what to expect and couldn't put it down."
  - M.M.M.

"Like James Herriot, but more magical!"
  - S.B.J.

The Dragon Doc Tales, Book 1: Wings and Wounds

Hi, I'm Doc, a veterinarian who sees dogs and cats, but also happens to see rather unusual patients: dragons. If this sounds unlikely to you, I can't blame you, but it's true. If you'd asked me years ago, I would have confidently said that dragons don't exist. Yet, here we are.

Dragons are nothing like what we've been taught. In truth, they try to avoid humans, and their hoards are... not what you'd think. Dragons are intelligent but not infallible creatures, and are just as prone to injuries and diseases as other, more domestic animals. That's where I come in. But as patients, dragons are, shall we say, a bit more challenging than dogs and cats. Just ask me how much burn cream I go through.

Join me as I recall my adventures—er, misadventures— in dragon medicine. From my first chance encounter with a dragon on a mountain to my panic when dragons visit my clinic; from the introduction of dragons to my staff and family to my harrowing flirtation with death, and all the near catastrophes along the way... let's just say, life with dragons is never dull.

www.ingramcontent.com/pod-product-compliance
Lightning Source LLC
Chambersburg PA
CBHW031550310726
48971CB00008B/2702